This book belongs to

_____

Walt Disney® VOLUME 6

REAL-LIFE
MONSTERS

WALT DISNEY FUN-TO-LEARN LIBRARY

A BANTAM BOOK
TORONTO • NEW YORK • LONDON • SYDNEY

"Wow, look at that dragon, Goofy," said Mickey. "What a huge tail and what pointed scales! The dragon is breathing fire and smoke! He has a mouth full of teeth and paws full of claws. He even has wings!"

Is there such a creature in the real-life world?

No. Dragons live only in fairy tales.

But people give the names *dragons* and *monsters* to some real creatures that seem scary to them.

Mickey and Goofy are about to look for some real-life monsters. Let's see how many strange and wonderful animals they can find.

Millions of years ago there lived animals called dinosaurs. The name *dinosaur* means "terrible lizard." Many dinosaurs looked like giant lizards. And they must have looked and sounded "terrible" to the smaller animals that lived many years ago.

"Gawrsh! Look at the size of that bone!" said Goofy, looking at a really large one in the museum.

"That's a Brontosaurus bone," said Mickey. "Brontosaurus was one of the biggest animals that ever lived."

Try to imagine an animal as long as six cars put together and as tall as a two-story house! Yet Brontosaurus was harmless to other animals. All it ate was plants. And that long neck must have sometimes been useful to it for reaching its food.

Just like today's animals, some dinosaurs ate plants, and some ate other animals.

Brachiosaurus was another huge dinosaur that ate only plants. It was so huge that it couldn't move fast enough to escape Allosaurus, a fierce dinosaur that ate other animals.

Allosaurus was about half the size of Brachiosaurus, but it had no trouble attacking the gentle giant with its daggerlike teeth and claws.

"Aw," said Goofy. "Poor old Brachiosaurus."

"Oh, I'll bet that guy with horns was scary," said Goofy. "It looks like a huge rhinoceros."

"It only looked fierce," said Mickey. "It was a plant eater."

Triceratops had two big horns on top of its head and one on the end of its nose. Its thick skin and horns helped to protect it from fierce meat-eating dinosaurs.

Plesiosaurus has been called the dragon of the seas of dinosaur times. These huge sea lizards had long, snaky necks and jaws full of sharp teeth. Their flippers helped them to swim.

They must have been a terror to other sea animals.

But not to Archelon and other ancient turtles. Archelon was a giant sea turtle that weighed as much as an elephant.

It's easy to remember the Stegosaurus because of the huge "plates" rising high off its backbone.

Stegosaurus was as long as the longest crocodile. Its hips were as high as the walls of a room. It was a peaceful, plant-eating animal, but it could defend itself well with a swish of its spiked tail.

"I sure wouldn't want to get caught near him!" said Goofy.

Dimetrodon was a meat eater that was about as big as an elephant. The sail on its back made it look even bigger! That strange sail may have taken in heat from the sun's rays to help keep its body warm. Or maybe it helped Dimetrodon keep its balance in the swampy land where it walked.

"It would have made a great sailboat," chuckled Goofy.

Pterosaurs were dinosaurs that could fly.

Sometimes they are called winged lizards.

Some pterosaurs were no bigger than crows. But this big pterosaur was a monster, with sharp teeth in its long beak and a huge bony skull.

"It looks like it's wearing a strange-looking bonnet," said Mickey.

Pterosaurs didn't have feathers. Their wings were flaps of skin, a little like the wings of a bat.

This terrifying monster was one of the last
of the great dinosaurs. It is called
Tyrannosaurus rex.

It had teeth like steak knives, and it was
as tall as a two-story house.

"It was the king of dinosaurs," said Mickey.

"Gawrsh, I wouldn't want to meet one,"
replied Goofy.

"Oh, no, Goofy," said Mickey, laughing.
"Tyrannosaurus rex, and all the other
dinosaurs, disappeared from earth long, long
ago. But do you know what, Goofy? We're
going to look for some real-life monsters
that are still alive today."

So Mickey and Goofy set out on a trip
to see how many they could find.

"Here," said Mickey, "is one very large animal that
even looks like a dinosaur or a storybook dragon. But really,
it's a very big lizard."

The Komodo dragon is a very long animal. It has a long neck,
a long body, long claws, a long tongue, and an especially long tail.
It can easily knock down a goat or a dog or a pig with a swipe of its
strong, heavy tail.

The Komodo uses its sharp teeth and claws to catch other animals.
But it has no wings, and it does not breathe fire and smoke.

The Komodo dragon is big and frightening.

But most lizards are small and harmless. One tiny lizard is no bigger than a dime. It's called a dwarf gecko.

"*Yeow!*" said Goofy, starting to run.

"It's all right, Goofy," said Mickey. "It's only a lizard! It won't hurt you!"

Imagine a harmless creature that can frighten away people or large, brave animals!

How does it do it?

The frilled lizard has a kind of collar, or ruff, of skin and bone around its neck. When it is angry or scared, the lizard raises its ruff. It opens its mouth in a wide, pink yawn. And suddenly it looks twice its normal size!

The chameleon isn't very large, but to many insects it looks like a real-life monster—if they see it in time!

This chameleon had picked a shady spot on a tree branch. It clutched the branch with its feet and sat very still.

Goofy rubbed his eyes and looked closer. The lizard's color had changed to match the color of the branch. The chameleon had almost disappeared!

Inside the lizard's mouth, its tongue was coiled up like a spring. As soon as a tasty-looking insect landed nearby, out shot the chameleon's tongue, catching the insect on its sticky tip.

The horned toad is not a toad. It is a lizard that lives
in the desert. Horned toads are squat-shaped, like toads, and
have "horns" on their heads, and spikes and warts on their
bodies.

One of them puffed itself up to frighten Goofy away.
Another scurried away to hide itself under a rock.

Sometimes horned toads use a special trick when they are
scared. They squirt what looks like blood from the corners
of their eyes! To an enemy, this is frightening indeed!
But horned toads are harmless, except to the insects they like
to eat.

Most lizards, except the Komodo dragon, have no large teeth or claws. But the Gila monster and the Mexican beaded lizard use poison to kill the small animals they need for food. They are the only poisonous lizards in the world. But even they are not really "monsters."

They live in the desert and are very shy, like most wild creatures. They look like brightly colored beaded bags.

Look what Pluto found. The fringe-toed lizard has "sandshoes"—it can skitter over loose sand. When it saw Pluto, this harmless little lizard closed its nostrils, dove deep into the sand, and "swam," paddling with its feet and tail.

"Sorry, Pluto, that's one trick you can't learn," said Mickey, laughing.

While Mickey and Goofy were outside their tent one hot
afternoon, a friendly animal came to join them. It was a large,
green lizard with a long, green tail.

"That's an iguana," said Mickey. "Iguanas often live in
people's houses. They eat up all the insects."

"Pretty handy to have around," said Goofy.

Sea iguanas are much bigger than land iguanas.
They live on islands far out at sea.
Sometimes they are called sea lizards. They dive underwater
and nibble on seaweeds.

Hundreds of sea iguanas crowd together on rocky islands
to bask in the sun and warm up after their swim.

Geckos chirrup to each other in a friendly way, especially at night. They cling onto the ceiling with the special sticky pads on their toes. Goofy thought he'd like to run around upside down, too.

"Wow, I didn't know lizards could water-ski," said Goofy. "And without a boat, too!"

A plumed basilisk had raised itself on its two hind legs and was dashing across the water. It didn't run very far. Soon it started to go under, and then it started to swim.

"That's a great escape trick!" said Mickey.

There are no dragons or monsters among animals.
But Mickey and Goofy found some giants!
Pythons and boas are the giants of the snake world.
If you could only get this python to stand straight up, it
would measure the length of four Goofys lined up end to end!
"I don't think I'll try it," thought Mickey.

Some snakes kill by using poison. A python kills a rat or another small creature by wrapping its coils around the animal and squeezing it until it cannot breathe anymore.

Most snakes don't take care of their little ones. But python mothers (and sometimes fathers, too) coil around their eggs and stay nearby until the eggs hatch. After that, the babies take care of themselves.

"That huge snake is a boa constrictor," said Mickey. "It's very, very large and long, but it won't hurt anybody unless it's hungry."

This boa has just had a meal. You can still see the bulge in its body. The boa is very sleepy and happy now. It will rest, quietly, for about a week. And then—watch out!

"Did you know that snakes can swallow animals bigger than their own mouths?" asked Mickey. "Their jawbones have a special 'hinge' that lets them open their mouths very wide. The skin around the snake's throat stretches like a rubber band. A snake can even swallow its food without chewing it!"

Have you ever seen a snake flick its tongue in and out? The snake uses its tongue as a special feeler to sense what is going on around it. That's how it finds its food.

Some snakes use poison to kill their food. The rattlesnake is a poisonous snake with a special trick. The "buttons" on the end of its tail make a strange rattling sound, which sometimes warns people and animals away.

But there are many snakes that do no harm, except to the insects and small animals they like to eat.

The king snake is a long, long snake, but it won't hurt you
at all. This king snake helps keep poisonous rattlesnakes and rats
and mice away from houses.

"Well, he's called a king snake," said Goofy, " so don't you
think he ought to have a crown?"

"Why not," replied Mickey, chuckling. "He's my favorite
snake, too."

"We can cross the river using these logs," said Mickey.
"I see a log floating in the water," said Goofy. "I'll hop onto it."
They looked closely into the water. They saw large eyes and
the twitch of a long tail. Suddenly a huge mouth, full of sharp
teeth, opened wide. The "log" was an alligator!
"*Yeow!*" shouted Goofy as he leaped quickly to the riverbank.
"That's the first time I ever saw a log with teeth!"

The crocodile looks very much like its cousin the alligator.
Both alligators and crocodiles are good mothers. The
crocodile builds her nest and guards her eggs carefully.

When the hatchlings come out of their shells, the mother
helps them out of the nest. She carries the babies in her
mouth, and takes them to the water.

Then she stays around for a few days and lets the babies
ride on her back.

Turtles move very, very slowly. But then, wouldn't you, if you had a heavy shell on your back and a hard covering underneath?

The little box turtle drew in its head and legs and was completely covered by its shell. "Where has it gone?" asked Goofy.

Turtles are usually harmless. Many turtles have long claws, but they won't hurt you. Only the snapping turtle may be dangerous if you get close enough.

Most seagoing turtles travel for thousands of miles around the oceans. But they have to come ashore to lay their eggs. The amazing thing is that they come back to the same place, year after year, to lay their eggs in the place where they were born.

The big mother turtle digs a hole in the sand, where the eggs won't be covered by water. Then she goes back to sea.

When the babies hatch, they climb out of the nest and walk toward the water. It's difficult for them to walk on land, because they have to use their flippers as legs. Then off they swim.

"What's the difference between a frog and a toad?" asked
Goofy.

"A frog is usually more lively than a toad," said Mickey.
"So it leaps and goes *plop!* into the pond before you can
catch it."

A toad spends more time away from water. It moves more
slowly. Its skin may have little raised spots called warts.

You may often hear frogs long before you can spot them. Frogs cheep, twitter, croak, and make loud booming sounds, especially on warm summer evenings. Bullfrogs have large sacs under their chins. They blow up these sacs like balloons when they boom. The sound may attract other frogs — or it may warn them to keep away. And sometimes, perhaps, the frogs are just talking to each other.

Most of the animals Mickey and Goofy saw on their adventures lay leathery-skinned eggs on land.

But frogs and toads have to find water when it's time to lay their eggs. Their babies, called tadpoles, must have water in which to grow.

"These can't be frog babies," said Goofy, staring at the wiggly creatures in the pond.

"Oh, yes, they are," said Mickey. "They look strange now, with their big heads and long tails. But soon their tails will get shorter and legs will appear. And one day, they'll find they must come out of the water to breathe. Those funny-looking tadpoles will have made the amazing change to frog or toad."

"*Yeow!*" yelled Goofy.

When Mickey and Goofy got home at last, Goofy wanted to know more about the creatures of the past.

But what kind of monster is this?

"Well," he said, when he saw Mickey laughing. "I forgot there's no such thing as a monster."

"That's right, Goofy," said Mickey. "Monsters live only in storybooks. Most real animals aren't even scary, once you find out about them. What adventures we've had, getting to know them!"